A NOTE TO PARENTS

When your children are ready to "step into reading," giving them the right books—and lots of them—is as crucial as giving them the right food to eat. **Step into Reading Books** present exciting stories or information reinforced with lively, colorful illustrations that make learning to read fun, satisfying, and worthwhile. They are priced so that acquiring an entire library of them is affordable. And they are beginning readers with an important difference—they're written on three levels.

Step 1 Books, with their very large type and extremely simple vocabulary, have been created for the very youngest readers. **Step 2 Books** are both longer and slightly more difficult. **Step 3 Books,** written to mid-second-grade reading levels, are for the child who has acquired even greater reading skills.

Children develop at different ages. **Step into Reading Books,** with their three levels of reading, are designed to help children become good—and interested—readers *faster.* The grade levels assigned to the three steps—preschool through grade 1 for Step 1, grades 1 through 3 for Step 2, and grades 2 and 3 for Step 3—are intended only as guides. Some children move through all three steps very rapidly; others climb the steps over a period of several years. These books will help your child "step into reading" in style!

Foghorn Island

Sea Witches

Ragged Reef

Lone Point

Copyright © 1988 by Geoffrey Hayes. All rights reserved under International and Pan-American Copyright Conventions. Published in the United States by Random House, Inc., New York, and simultaneously in Canada by Random House of Canada Limited, Toronto.

Library of Congress Cataloging-in-Publication Data:
Hayes, Geoffrey. The secret of Foghorn Island / by Geoffrey Hayes. p. cm. — (Step into reading. A step 3 book) SUMMARY: Otto and Uncle Tooth, detectives, investigate a series of shipwrecks, which brings them in touch with the dangerous Sid Rat. ISBN: 0-394-89614-9 (pbk.); 0-394-99614-3 (lib. bdg.) [1. Mystery and detective stories. 2. Sea stories. 3. Animals—Fiction.] I. Title. II. Series: Step into reading. Step 3 book. PZ7.H31455Sf 1988 [E]—dc 19 87-16095 CIP AC

Manufactured in the United States of America 1 2 3 4 5 6 7 8 9 0

STEP INTO READING is a trademark of Random House, Inc.

Step into Reading

THE SECRET OF FOGHORN ISLAND

by Geoffrey Hayes

A Step 3 Book

Boogle Bay

Random House 🏠 New York

Otto and his uncle Tooth were
detectives. Their motto was

NO MYSTERY TOO DEEP,

NO ADVENTURE TOO SCARY.

One night Jack Whiskers sent for
them. He was at the inn with Captain
Poopdeck.

4

"Yesterday I was in my boat," said Jack Whiskers. "I was bringing a golden bell to Boogle Bay for the town hall.

"It was very foggy. Suddenly I saw a dark shadow float over me in the sky.

"Before I could tell what it was, a storm came up.

"My boat hit Ragged Reef, and I was thrown onto the rocks. When I came to, the storm was gone. So was the golden bell!

"My boat had a big hole in it, but I jumped into my life raft and escaped."

"This is the fourth shipwreck in a month," said Captain Poopdeck. "Something strange is going on. We need someone to find the bell and solve the mystery."

Uncle Tooth puffed on his pipe. "Otto and I will do it," he said. "We will take our boat to Ragged Reef and look for clues."

"That might be dangerous," said Jack Whiskers.

"Danger is our middle name," said Otto.

A stranger was listening at a table nearby. When he had heard enough, he crept away.

The next morning Otto and Uncle
Tooth were getting their boat, the
Courage, ready to sail.

Auntie Hick walked up the gangway.
"I'm coming with you," she said.

"Don't be silly," said Uncle Tooth.
"You will be better off at home."
"Someone has to cook hot meals
for Otto," said Auntie Hick.

She opened her carpetbag and brought out a wool cap.

"I made this for Otto so he won't catch cold," she said.

She pushed the cap down on his head.

"I feel stupid wearing this," said Otto.

"Stuff and nonsense!" said Auntie Hick.

"I guess we are stuck with her," Uncle Tooth whispered.

They saw a stranger rolling a barrel along the dock.

"Pardon me," the stranger said. "My name is Mr. Tar. I must take this barrel of cheese to my sick grandmother. Can you give me a lift to Lone Point?"

"Sure," said Uncle Tooth.

They helped Mr. Tar roll the barrel
on board. They stored it in the cabin.

"Meet Auntie Hick, our cook," said
Uncle Tooth.

"Hello. I will have eggs and toast
for lunch," said Mr. Tar.

"The nerve!" said Auntie Hick.

Soon it was time to leave. Uncle
Tooth pulled in the gangway. Otto
raised the anchor.

Captain Poopdeck and Jack Whiskers
came by to see them off.

"Good luck!" they called.

The Courage left the harbor for
the open sea. The waves were frisky.
The sky was full of gulls.

Mr. Tar sat on a crate and watched Uncle Tooth steer the boat.

"Do not go past Foghorn Island," he warned. "Sea monsters live near there. I do not want them to eat me or my cheese."

Uncle Tooth snorted.

"Otto and I are not afraid of sea monsters."

After a while, Mr. Tar got up.

"The salt air makes me dizzy," he said. "I think I will go lie down."

Auntie Hick was busy cooking eggs.

She did not trust Mr. Tar. She wondered if there really was cheese inside his barrel.

She bent down and put her eye to a knothole.

Another eye looked back at her!

The lid of the barrel flew off. Out
popped a weasel with a knife between
his teeth.

Auntie Hick screamed. Then she
saw Mr. Tar.

He had a gun in one paw and a
sword in the other.

Mr. Tar and the weasel grabbed Auntie Hick and dragged her out on deck.

"Mr. Tar! What are you doing?" said Otto.

Mr. Tar took off his hat and dark glasses.

"Sid Rat's the name!" he snarled. "Robbery is my game! We are taking your boat. If you try to stop us, we will feed Auntie Hick to the sharks."

"There are no sharks in these waters," said Uncle Tooth.

Sid Rat laughed.

"Good. Then Auntie Hick will drown in peace."

"All right. You win," said Uncle Tooth.

Sid Rat made Otto and Uncle Tooth climb inside the cheese barrel.

"Auntie Hick is coming with us to be our cook," he told them. "But you boys are getting off here."

He pushed the barrel into the water.

"Don't worry, Auntie Hick. Uncle Tooth and I will rescue you," called Otto.

"Har! Har! Sure you will!" cried Sid Rat.

The robbers took off.

Otto and Uncle Tooth were left alone in the cold sea.

"Look!" cried Uncle Tooth.

He pointed to a hot-air balloon. It was moving toward them.

"Help! Save us!" they yelled.

The balloon sailed over the barrel.
Suddenly there was a bolt of lightning.
Wind began to blow. Rain poured down.
    Big waves smashed the barrel
against Ragged Reef. Otto and Uncle
Tooth jumped out.

They hid behind some rocks.
The balloon sailed away.
The storm went with it.
"This is a fine kettle of fish,"
moaned Otto.

"We aren't licked yet," said Uncle Tooth. "We can use all this wreckage to build a new boat."

"But we don't have any nails," said Otto.

"We don't need nails. We will tie the boards together with rope," said Uncle Tooth.

They set to work.

Before long their boat was finished.

"It's not very pretty," said Uncle
Tooth. "But it floats. Let's call it the
Courage Two."

"Good idea," said Otto. "Where are
we going?"

"To Foghorn Island, of course," said
Uncle Tooth. "That is where the
robbers took Auntie Hick."

"How do we know that?" said Otto.

Uncle Tooth chewed on his pipe.

"Because that is the one place Sid
Rat told us to stay away from."

They passed a group of Sea
Witches. Otto drew a little closer to his
uncle.

"Are you sure we aren't afraid of
sea monsters?" he whispered.

"Sure I'm sure," said Uncle Tooth.
He tipped his hat.

"Excuse me, ladies," he called.
"Could you lead us to Foghorn Island?"

One of the witches swam forward.

"What will you give me?" she asked.

Uncle Tooth held up his pipe.

"How about this?" he asked.

"I already have a pipe," said the Sea Witch.

"How about my cap?" asked Otto.
"It's a deal," said the Sea Witch.
Otto tossed his cap to her.
It fit perfectly.

The Sea Witch dove underwater.
She came up with a long strand of
seaweed.

"Grab the other end," she said.

Uncle Tooth got a good grip on the
seaweed.

The witch put it between her teeth
and pulled the boat across the waves.

After a time, the air became thick
and dark. They could just see
Foghorn Island through the gloom.

"What a scary-looking place," said
Otto.

The Sea Witch let go of the seaweed.

"Thanks," said Uncle Tooth. "You have been a big help."

The Sea Witch tipped her cap and swam away.

Otto and Uncle Tooth steered the Courage Two to shore.

Then they walked along the beach.
It was cold and damp.

Suddenly lightning flashed.

The hot-air balloon floated down to
the island and disappeared behind some
rocks.

Otto and Uncle Tooth ran after it.

A man with bushy hair tied the
balloon to a tall tree. Then he climbed
down a rope ladder.

"See where he goes," whispered
Uncle Tooth. "I want to get a closer
look at that balloon."

Otto nodded.

He followed the glow of the man's lantern through the fog.

Soon they came to a cove. The Courage was anchored there, safe and sound!

The lights in the cabin were lit.
Smoke was coming out of the chimney.

The man with bushy hair walked up
the gangway and into the cabin.

Otto tiptoed after him.

Otto peeked in a porthole.

Auntie Hick was frying fish.

Sid Rat, the weasel, and the man
with bushy hair were seated at the
table.

They were counting a pile
of treasure. On top of the pile was
the golden bell for the town hall!

"Your weather balloon will make us
rich, Doctor Ocular," said Sid Rat.

"Indeed it will," agreed the doctor.
"And now we have this fine boat
to store our loot in."

"Hurry up with that chow, woman!"
Sid Rat yelled to Auntie Hick.

Auntie Hick was so angry she burned the fish.

"Just wait. Otto and Uncle Tooth will capture you thieves," she said.

"No chance of that," said Doctor Ocular. "I left them stranded on Ragged Reef!"

Otto ran to the door.

"That's what you think!" he cried.

"Get him!" screamed Sid Rat.

The robbers chased Otto across the deck and down the gangway.

Otto ran as fast as his legs could carry him, but Sid Rat was close behind.

There was a flash of lightning. Otto looked up.

Uncle Tooth was in the weather balloon!

He found a button that said RAIN. When he pressed it, water came pouring down.

The robbers got soaking wet.

"This is fun," said Uncle Tooth.

He pressed a button that said THUNDER. There was a loud boom.

The robbers screamed and ran down the beach. Uncle Tooth followed them.

The robbers saw the Courage Two.
They climbed onto it.

Uncle Tooth pressed the WIND
button.

WHOOSH!

A huge gust of wind blew the
robbers out to sea.

Uncle Tooth climbed down the rope ladder and jumped onto the beach.

The weather balloon sailed off into the fog.

"Without the balloon there will be no more strange shipwrecks," said Uncle Tooth. "The mystery is solved!"

He walked back to the Courage.

Otto and Auntie Hick were on deck.

"Auntie Hick, didn't I tell you Uncle Tooth and I would rescue you?" said Otto.

"Never mind that. I want to know what happened to your cap," said Auntie Hick.

Otto told her.

"Well, I never!" she said.

When they left the island, they saw Sid Rat, the weasel, and Doctor Ocular sitting on a rock in the middle of the ocean.

They were talking to the Sea Witch.

"What will you give me if I help you escape?" she asked.

"My cap?" asked Sid Rat.

"Sorry, I already have a cap," said the Sea Witch.

Uncle Tooth laughed.

"That should hold those crooks for a while."

When Otto, Uncle Tooth, and Auntie Hick came back to Boogle Bay, they were heroes.

Auntie Hick said she never wanted to go on another sea voyage again. She went home to knit Otto a new cap.

The golden bell was placed atop the town hall.

Otto was allowed to ring it for the first time.

"It sounds truly golden," said Jack Whiskers.

Everyone from miles around came to see it. Everyone but Sid Rat and his gang.

The next day Otto was digging
for clams. He saw a hot-air balloon
drift over Boogle Bay. He looked through
his spyglass.

He thought he could see Sid Rat,
Doctor Ocular, and the weasel inside.

But before he could get a closer
look, the balloon disappeared.